this is what it feels like

this is what it feels like

edited by
Julia Prendergast and Rebekah Clarkson

This is What it Feels Like
Recent Work Press
Canberra, Australia

Copyright © the authors, 2025

ISBN: 9781764106832 (paperback)

A catalogue record for this
book is available from the
National Library of Australia

Cover image: *Embrace* (Indian ink and charcoal on drafting film, 2024),
          by Margaret Ambridge, used with permission.
Cover design: Recent Work Press
Set by Recent Work Press

recentworkpress.com

Contents

Introduction

We're in Singapore. It's 2023.

Julia Prendergast, Shady Cosgrove, Gay Lynch and Billie Travalini are speaking on 'The Importance of Flash Fiction' at the 16th International Conference of the Short Story in English, hosted by the National Institute of Education, Nanyang Technological University. It's a vibrant discussion from generous minds. I am in the audience. I watch as these writers keep tabs on who has spoken least, invite each other in, weave and twist. They share creative process, debate the meaninglessness of genre in their own practice, dismiss commercial viability. I notice their open sandalled feet crossed neatly at ankles underneath the long table as they read their work aloud: very short stories that are provocative, funny, subversive, and moving. This is storytelling where everything is working, and every paragraph break carries, as Shady notes, its own 'urgency'. Listening to the discussion, I am reminded of the *unusual joy*[1] inherent in wrangling a whole world into a small, small space—of creative confinement—of creating puzzles that insist on being solved.

I miss this feeling—*unusual joy*—as a writer.

I have a simple idea: A flash fiction writing group with these four writers. I propose—apropos of nothing—a visual prompt-based writing group.

They all say: *Yes*.

Over the course of the following year, we will each alternate emailing the group a visual prompt to inspire new stories (I suggest up to 300 words). There will be no deadlines, no sharing of writing, no feedback, no obligations beyond sending an image prompt. I don't want to add more obligation to these obligation-laden writers.

The visionary amongst us—Julia Prendergast—who sees things before others, leans in and says quietly, *You know this is a book, Clarkson*. I don't, but she plants the seed.

Two things happen, neither of which I anticipate.

The first: a small and generous community emerges. While there is little correspondence between prompts, each one generates a flurry of responses that speak to serendipity, comfort, productivity, and that elusive joy—*I love receiving these and being connected to you all; The lack of pressure, sense of community, prompts and parameters have all conspired to get me writing with joy, not with obligation or angst, and for this I am grateful to you all.*

There are no consequences if an image falls flat, if life is too complicated to facilitate the generation of an *outcome.* Why does this feel revolutionary?

We don't share our stories—I am strangely emphatic about this. I've become curious about the idea of writers sharing images that might build a natural collective consciousness, without the influence of seeing one another's work.

Images arrive with brief references to our lives and preoccupations. Billie's desire to send an image of the aqueduct in Segovia, Spain, is delayed, the photograph stored in a house she cannot easily access. Julia, hard pressed for time, grabs a shot of a precious postcard from Poros, Greece, which is stuck to her desktop. Shady sends a photograph of her open fridge during a hectic weekend of overseas visitors. Billie sends a painting of a Union Soldier in the Delaware regiment. There is a Rothko forgery, an old sepia image of maternal ancestors, a picture of Margaret Atwood, a teeming crowd, a jellyfish.

We think carefully upon the images, or not at all. There is no overarching theme, although serendipity abounds.

Gay sends a photograph of a bright orange fox, leaping in crisp air, hovering over snow-covered ground. I dream about a fox pelt, but I can't *find* the story. Gay breaks 'the rule' of one prompt and sends a suite of four. Her anarchy inspires the obvious realisation that the images can intersect and overlap, solve provocations, or intensify a koan. Early one morning a bolt of colour catches my eye at the top of the driveway. A fox. Skinny, auburn, fleeting. Where I live, on Peramangk land, we have possums, rodents and rabbits, but I've never seen a fox.

Now foxes are everywhere.

Then I encounter Margaret Ambridge's artwork, 'Embrace'. It's part of a collaborative exhibition with South Australian writer Carol Lefevre, at the launch of Carol's book on ageing, *Bloomer* (Affirm Press, 2025).

'Embrace' will become our cover artwork. It also becomes the final visual prompt sent to each writer. We are indebted to the generosity of this gifted artist, and to the fortuity so often encountered in the pursuit of art.

The second thing that happens is that Julia Prendergast is right—this is a book—partly because she makes it so—submitting an early manuscript to the brilliant Shane Strange, publisher at Recent Work Press. She also offers to co-edit. I am honoured to have collaborated with Julia to bring *This is What it Feels Like* to fruition. I am deeply grateful for her unrelenting rigour and generosity of spirit and mind.

As our prompt-based writing year came to an end, I was curious to see each writer's ekphrastic responses, but also to see what may have occurred—quietly and covertly—across the responses. Indeed, a collective consciousness had emerged, not just across the stories, but *between* them—in the 'empty' spaces—with an energy more likely to reverberate in story-cycles and composite forms, than in anthologies. We had become a community and so had our stories.

As we collected the stories together, we also understood that the images had lost their relevance. Their absence had become, as Julia noted, a 'ghostly space to be navigated by the reader via the concrete and specific details of the words on the page.'

Ekphrastic responses to the images fed, and were fed by, other writing projects. They stimulated autobiographical writing, experimentation, fiction. In an interview in *The Paris Review*, Helen Garner speaks of the compulsion to write when she senses her experiences form into the 'kind of curve' known as a 'story' (2022: p. 132). 'Story is a chunk of life with a bend in it,' she says (2022: p. 132). The same may be said for the pieces in *This is What it Feels Like,* however you might define them.

What doesn't surprise me is that the words 'mother' and 'mum' occur fifty-eight times across the book. Vixens abound.

Books tend to show us, through their language and structure, how to read them. My hope is that *This is What it Feels Like* does this for you. We invite you not to read these stories as a random collection by five writers—not even as 'independent' stories that are 'interdependent' when read together, as story cycles go—but as independently written stories that speak to our innate *interdependence* as human beings. And as

Julia adds, to our 'sense of ourselves as a plurality of selves.'

I have taken great pleasure in arranging the stories in the order they appear—considering the echoing effect, and the 'network of associations' found in story cycles that are both subtle and cumulative (Luscher, 1989: p. 149). I've also tried to honour each story as its own 'apocalypse, served in a very small cup' not wanting to 'bump' any of them against their 'neighbours' and inadvertently 'do them harm' (Hortense Calisher in Luscher, 1989: p. 148).

We encourage you to enjoy the stories in *This is What it Feels Like* in the order in which they appear.

But also, do whatever the hell you want.

Rebekah Clarkson (on behalf of the co-editors)

References

Garner, H. (2022, Fall). The Art of Fiction No. 255. *The Paris Review, 241,* 128–156.
Luscher, R. M. (1989). The short story sequence: An open book. In S. Lohafer & J. E. Clarey (Eds.), *Short Story Theory at a Cross-roads* (pp. 148–167). Louisiana State University Press.

[1]While shared in a different context, I thank Eva Hornung for this phrase.

Aphids

Should I cut the ivy before I leave? Rescue the aphids clusterfucking the stem? Aphids are attracted to young, tender, fast-growing plant parts, rich in nitrogen. They also like stressed plants. I close the browser.

Julia Prendergast

The Road Trip

My husband appeared from the walk-in robe wearing his Top Gun leather jacket from 1988. We'd been married thirty-two years and while I hadn't seen it for most of those, I remembered the jacket well, its stonewashed patina, faux military patches, scent of animal and musk.

'When I bought this,' he said, slipping his hands into the pockets, 'the guy in the shop said that this was the sort of jacket you put on the backseat when you go on a road trip.' My husband pursed his mouth, furrowed his brow and pulled in his bottom lip.

'I've never been on a road trip,' he said, shaking his head slowly.

'Are you going to wear it?' I asked, hoping he'd say yes, watching from our bed, as my husband undertook the final stages of packing. He had no real plans, only a booking for tonight in a motel three hours away, and a line-up of earnest podcasts about the Roman Empire, which he insisted was about everything, in the end.

I remembered my friend's photograph of the Segovia Aqueduct, how she had inferred something similar.

'Maybe, wearing that jacket, you'll meet someone in a bar,' I said, though my husband had never flirted in his life.

'That's *not* going to happen,' he said. Whether he had no confidence in his abilities, or infidelity was inconceivable, I wasn't completely sure.

'Well, if you do,' I said, 'let me know, so I can quickly meet someone too.' He grimaced, as he often did, when I pushed him like this.

I stood barefoot in the driveway under a shadowed sun and watched him reverse out of our driveway. I wondered what and who he would find, whether I would be here when he returned.

Rebekah Clarkson

Remembering Civilisation

We stand outside ancient ruins. The hostel has dirty bathrooms but clean beds and this seems a fair compromise. We don't have a son yet. We haven't bought a house, in fact the notion of a mortgage seems quietly thrilling. We count our euros and wait for the tour, held in a language (we think) we understand. You don't hold my hand, but I haven't noticed that yet. You tell me about the weather, the cricket, your mother, and I am interested.

Shady Cosgrove

Rewilding

London swelters in early summer. Her baby idles on his back, belly exposed, drops of sweat glistening on his brow. Inside the wicker basket beside her bed, her hand rises and falls on his chest. As she dozes, warm air shifts in curtain billow.

A downstairs crash scatters her dreams of old workplaces. Hard scrabble noises jerk her awake. Fuck's sake, is this a home invasion? She speed-dials.

From his refrigerated Brugge apartment, her partner soothes her.

'Don't open windows while I'm gone.' Incompetent little expat, in parenthesis.

From the first-floor landing, her brain calibrates clicks as they cross the kitchen floor. She charges downstairs to find a stainless-steel bin upended.

A red burnished streak launches itself through an open hopper window, lands and turns to hold her gaze. A vixen perhaps, with hungry cubs, a yellow-eyed, desperate raider, she's been watching. A creature of the night boldly taking its chance at midday.

In liminal light, London foxes slide in and out of view, pass through gardens, to dance on moonlit commons. Once, from the upstairs nursery, she had seen one asleep, in long grass in her neighbour's yard, its body curved around cubs. Suburban dissonance. A foreign city-mother at rest in an unfrequented rear garden.

Back home, foxes tear out the eyes of newborn lambs, snatch sweetmeats from the sides of poultry, strew them, pull bleeding broken birds through fences, take great bites of flesh—then flee. Farmers string them along fence lines, like handmaids hung from the wall to salvage Gilead. Foxes and women, head wounds, rope burns.

She pushes her pram past unkempt blocks of flats. A bushy-tailed animal lies splayed on the grass. Its haunted, vulpine face shattered by a bullet, one mile from the Thames, yards from the High Street, a lifetime from an English turf war.

Gay Lynch

Twentieth Century Fox

Selma Betterfield looks in the mirror at the deep creases at the corners of her mouth, imagines them crawling over her chin and settling in the form of flabby skin at the base of her neck. Her husband, LeRoy, is downstairs yelling something about wanting to be fed. Selma is *not* in the mood to talk about food, or anything else for that matter, so she keeps looking in the mirror and says, 'Goddamn it, where'd the years go?'

'Yo, are we gonna eat or what?' LeRoy exaggerates a South Philly accent, drawing out the *o* as if he's Rocky Balboa and *Yo* is a two-syllable word.

Selma resists the urge to laugh, knowing he'll more than likely interpret her laugh as proof she finds humour in being at his beck and call.

She wants him dead, sooner the better.

Still, she doesn't say anything. She closes her eyes and imagines she's twenty, with a tiny waist and thick hair fanning over her shoulders like one of those fluffy stoles they made out of dead foxes, back when fur farms dotted the landscape and wearing a dead animal on your shoulder was fashionable.

'Gorgeous,' onlookers would say, and pet the fox as if it were alive and pleased as punch to be getting so much attention, and a free ride to boot.

Selma thinks about all this and about an article she once read in National Geographic—Dmitry Belyaev, a Russian geneticist, bred foxes to discover how many generations it would take to produce a fox, house-trained as a French poodle.

'Ten generations,' she says, 'that's all. What about us?'

'Yo, Selma,' LeRoy yells.

Coming, she mouths, walking downstairs, one slow step at a time.

Billie Travalini

Relief

It will be a relief to be clear of the never-ending claustrophobia
of eggs frying, toast charring.

Julia Prendergast

This is What it Feels Like

You've known for five whole decades that this will happen, that your son will one day show up at your house. So many mornings, you have wondered, if it might be today.

There'll be other things, yes. Bills to pay, light bulbs to replace, scones to bake, grammar to correct, pianos to play, haircuts to endure, pantries to clean, fridges to stock, grandchildren to hold, mothers to imagine, men to remember, corners to dust. What you won't know, is that when it happens, when he finds you, there will be no knock on the door.

He will stand in front of your house. You will be walking through the lounge, and you will see him, fleetingly, through glass. You will know it is him.

Everything will come to this. Stillness.

You will wait it out in the kitchen; you will lean into the windowpane; you will pull yourself away. Your scalp will burn and there will be thunder in your ears, an open-cut mine in your mouth—fairy floss, a ferris-wheel, a freight-train.

Rebekah Clarkson

Strata Redevelopment Act

I've received the contract for Smith Street. Remember—you stayed here with me. Back and forth with lawyers, court. The sale's been forced. I watch my route to work now—grief for old houses, trees cut down ... How do the elderly go anywhere without crying?

Shady Cosgrove

Like Sisters

Wind turbines run the ridge, a wind farm atop the mountain's wave-like peaks, windvanes dancing like sisters, heads and arms in harmonic rhythm, beating a thrum to the wind's channels.

Julia Prendergast

Patience

A woman wearing a lace collar lives in your wardrobe. The collar looks out of place on this tall figure with strong hands. She doesn't speak, never leaves, but hums as she irons shirts and trousers, hanging them overhead. You've never seen her outside the closet, but she must venture into bedroom and kitchen—dishes get washed and the bed is always made. This woman is so tall for such a crowded space, doesn't smile for the camera, only offers an expression of impersonal kindness before getting on with getting things done. There's been a mistake, she should never have been hired, but here she is–waiting for family to grow, leave home– before she can slip away from the unwashed and into the great, when no one is watching.

Shady Cosgrove

A Small Hut by the Sea

In bushranger parlance, Myrtle's find might be described as a hide-out. For Myrtle, it is a small hut by the sea, and exactly—*miraculously*—as she had fantasised. She likes to push her bare feet into the boards to verify the stability of the floor.

Myrtle's prickling desire had been to pare back. Desire is not a strong enough word; hers was a ship-turning, tectonic plate-shifting, wordless, shapeless force. Myrtle could barely articulate what she had wanted removed—*removed*—from her orbit. All sentient beings. Yes, even animals. Most objects, though not her skeins of yarn, obviously.

Sound.

Myrtle wanted sound removed.

Never again did she wish to hear the slurping, swallowing sounds of anyone—*anyone*—in her vicinity. Coughing: no. Bird sound: tolerable. Calm tidal water: actually, yes. Only water, then.

Slowly, her project takes shape. Soon, she well understands, it will reach end-to-end of the hut and there'll be new decisions to make. Instinct-driven and impractical, the knitting project is now her sole interest.

Gulls soar overhead, quiet and majestic.

Myrtle misses her sisters, of course. Misses them in her bones. She silently recites their names: Rosalind, Mary, Nance, Maude, Lily. Her tongue flicks around the playful mix of her sisters' consonants and vowels, lapping the top of her mouth.

How has Myrtle failed to note the sensation of her own tongue in her own mouth? She snaps a plump pickleweed branch from her gathered stash and crunches the little pods against her teeth, splitting skin, tart-salty juice trickling down her throat.

She won't go back.

Rebekah Clarkson

Contrition

For thirty-plus years you let me assume, in big ways and small, each sofa-slept night was my fault—as if your logic in all things, except for storming the Capital and expecting me to applaud how you almost got to Pelosi, and you would have, if some Capital police officer hadn't told you to turn left when you should've turned right—as if turning left was your only mistake, and every other thing you ever did made perfectly good sense.

Billie Travalini

Fucksake

Fucksake. His moves. Our silences.

Julia Prendergast

My Mother Wants to Talk …

My mother wants to talk about her sister. My sister wants to talk about our mother. I don't want to talk to either of them about mothers or sisters.

We look at ourselves—looking at ourselves looking at ourselves.

Shady Cosgrove

Until then

We shuffle and roll our bodies, careful with our rawness, but also not careful. Fluorescents buzz and rubber wheels on metal legs skid across lino floors. Outside our windows, a January sun. Birds chirp and fuss in leaf litter, unperturbed by the birth of our babies. Later, when I have left and you have also left and it's as though that place never existed, the birds still chatter and rustle and trill—spoggies, magpies, blackbirds.

How fast the years go by. How many summers will I have? Autumns to imagine. Winters to endure. Springs to forget. We carry on. The world shifts and tilts. Around the sun I go. Around you go too. I know where you are; oh, I've always known. I know your new name, first and last.

Only decades later do I tell my sisters and my son. My husband never learns of you. I lie when people ask, as they always do: *How many children do you have?*

One, I tell them. *One son.*

Here is something I have learnt. If you suddenly and unexpectedly feel like crying, you should: tears will not always be free or willing. If you feel an uncomfortable prickling, a quiver of your lip, heat rising: surrender. Because here is something true. You will feel a little better afterward—in the way of the sand after the tide has come in, and the garden, after the rain.

Rebekah Clarkson

Betrayal

I never saw it coming.

Betrayal is silent, hiding in broad daylight, like a twisted road sign folding into itself.

Billie Travalini

After an Election

Margaret Atwood is my therapist. I lie on the couch, which is also a towel on the beach. We prefer being outside, without phones— no news. She passes the sunscreen and asks what I remember of oceans. It takes concentration but I tell her about the sound of waves at full tide. My brain fills with salt and white caps and flying fish that skim the water's surface. I tell her how I was on my surfboard, and they flew over-across-into me. God was in those scales and that glint of early sunlight. I was chosen, and all of my handmaid pain receded.

Shady Cosgrove

Delirium

I'm steeped in rainbow delirium—front-facing wits'-end-mothering—extended reckoning, memory's unflappable chorus.

Julia Prendergast

Leaving in Four

One

I come from a long line of women who hide their heads in the sand.

On being told that my father was having an affair with a younger, allegedly prettier version of my mother, my maternal grandmother advised her daughter: *Put your head in the sand, darling.*

I have only just been told this story.

Two

I want to see my friend, but I do not want to see her husband, not because I'm not fond of her husband—I am, and always have been—but because I need to have the kind of conversation women can only have when their husbands are not present. Everything is different without the husbands.

My friend says there's a lot to think about: *The whitegoods alone.*

Three

A relationship psychologist on Instagram says that if your needs are being met to the extent that you are able to grieve the needs that are not, then enough of your needs are being met.

Try saying that quickly.

Then ask: what are my needs? And: what does 'needs being met' mean?

Four

It is the second time I see the fox. I go out to the car in the morning alone and there it is, at the top of the driveway. Motionless. Its eyes pierce mine, and then it's gone.

Rebekah Clarkson

Never Enough

I think of home, my children, the sense of irreparable *responsibility* because I brought them into the world. The demented nature of that never-enough love.

Julia Prendergast

Red Brains: Red Games

Red manifests in amygdala and Mars. Over slow summers, furious flashpoints, fast fires. Scrubs ignite. Flames rampage right to the sea. One billion Australian animals burnt. Seven hot global seas: ours on record. Rivers rise, houses capsize: hard to measure on an MRI.

Human brains, heavy with clever dread, weigh down newborns, until one year hence, set on their feet, they snatch and jerk their own weight, balance on spine, shoulder, toes and perambulate forward for another decade, before inhaling newsbytes.

Amygdala tells us, beware the bear Krasny, Russian-red, hot beauty, latent heat and reckoning. Like Red Guards, worker blood, Rus people, Ruthenia. Red October, Romanov red. Soviet, Rubra.

Putin, puttin' a toe 'cross a red line to where nightingales, call out sweetly, ready to die, despite or because of a red button. On these terms, so-called West ready to let 'em. Whose book of revelations foreshadows this fuckening?

Who engorges on the colour red? Military money multiplies? Red-ragged by industrial complexes, red-faced men play with morte. Raise your hand if you're in. End game. Exchange your queens.

Boomer-fuel sky-high, real-estate through the roof; XYZ, Alpha no stable shelter, just doof. Like Jesus, who survived Herodes Magnus's census and sword. Unlike people smashed in Mariupol, fleeing beneath a blood moon.

Amygdala, red hot—COVID alarm goes off. Even asymptomatic brains shrink up to two per cent. Bad weather, precipitated by Donald, Joe, *Scomo*, Vlado, those hungry, thieving red foxes. Red-bum monkey allure, not ovulatory, phallocentric fear of power lost.

Do you believe greed pees blood, or that lies light up your arse, explode your brain, dilute good red, combust over patriarchal curses, that wrathful horsemen trample all the hope of getting out of this one?

28

Gay Lynch

Photo of a forgery

It's a living room gig, a square of stage next to the stairwell, mismatched chairs in front. The stained-glass lamp in the corner casts shadows through glass doors, towards the empty swimming pool. I follow the slanted darkness outside to wait for the toilet, watching the blank concrete, the diving board: swimming pools are eerie without water.

You were also waiting, talking to someone we both knew, searching your pockets with an urgency that made me want to know what you were looking for. Though of course that can't be true: we wouldn't meet for another five years—but still, I remember being introduced, your new sneakers, the laugh-talk of your voice. I remember diving into that pool, swimming the length of it after everyone had gone to bed.

Shady Cosgrove

A Scan of the Female Organs

Dr Andrew Daniels is seventy-one-years old, but he feels twenty-five. So, when his next patient presents, a fifty-year-old woman with lower abdominal pain, he cannot help but see her as a peer of his mother's. When she tells of a twenty-three-year-old daughter, he finds himself imagining the daughter as a younger, prettier version of the woman—this is only natural, for all young women are potential conquests to a virile man. He is compelled, then, to tell the woman his anecdote about Michael Brown, his best friend in high school who, for three reasons, took Home Economics instead of Economics. Dr Daniels counts the reasons, his fingers raised high to the woman's face. One: learn how to sew; two: learn how to cook; three: be the only boy among thirty-two girls.

Dr Daniels throws his head back, a raucous laugh, a quick eye to the woman. He starts to type, senses her watching his two-finger technique and explains that his mother had been a great touch typist, would type his notes from medical school, hand him the pages. A wink. And now, yes. Tummy pain, eh?

He will order an ultrasound, and she need only take the form to a pathology centre listed on the back. He says he will order a scan of the female organs.

Later, as the afternoon sun dips behind the red-tiled roof of the clinic, an ambulance wails nearby, though Dr Daniels, backing out of the clinic carpark, thinks nothing of it, glances happily at his empty lunch box tucked at the base of his passenger seat. He marvels at his capability throughout the day (retirement be damned!), thinks again of his dear mother, plans a sherry in his special chair, with the footstool.

Rebekah Clarkson

Pine Needles

I've been clocking my life in failed-mothering-moments, a mothering-police doom-scape—shame-memories spindled like clumps of pine needles, shoreside mounds, raked into piles by the wash.

What does it mean to be a GOOD mother?

Julia Prendergast

Delectatio

Between bedroom door hinges, view of Mother's breasts, flawless skin, yellowing, brought about by sunless confinement. Mothballs scattered across polished boards. Dust and naphthalene smells. Daughter inhales something else. Faint, fishy. Recognisable.

Naked before cheval mirror, Mother sways, utters small screeches. Eyes heavy and languid, entranced by something inaccessible to her watcher. She hauls the fox-fur stole from the cedar robe, to encircle her shoulders like a noose or retroverted womb. Its dessicated weight rests on her right breast. Its burnished tail exposes her left, fringes her elbow.

In mirror-glass reflection. Starved, murdered, skinned, heart and child-free vulpine creature. Shifts, shudders. Mother twitches, lifts gramophone needle, stuck on Bessie Smith, 'Backwater Blues'.

Nostalgic piano trills. Mother brings the soft fur to her mouth, licks her lips, pats hard vixen muzzle. Stole settles on narrow shoulders. Face attempts composure. Air redolent, perhaps, of Father's fee-for-service approaches, dowsing between her thighs.

Vixen, swift nocturnal, existential breeder. Trapped by fence and bullet, now tissue paper. Sans old stink of mange and shit.

Mother touches herself, moans softly, arms cradling the incurve of her belly, soft tracery behind which two sons flourished before they fled, first her body, then into construction, design, war.

Her fingers drop to stir unwaxed, nether hair, then rise to her nostrils, to inhale the rich smell, likely mixed with eau-de-parfum, Lily of the Valley.

The same scents waft from Daughter's fingers, as she bucks beneath bedcovers, reading Anaïs Nin.

Years ago, corseted in black crepe, had Mother refused Father luncheon in Rundle Street, remained at her music stand with manuscript sheet, set her metronome going, sung scales near the open door, until a pallid cuckoo picked up her melody?

'Come, I've run your bath,' Daughter calls, stepping into the room. 'Hand me your fox.'

Mother startles, turns. Covers flushed face with back of her hand. Mumbles *'voluptās*, voluptātis, voluptātī, voluptātem ...' Smiles. Releases fox at her feet.

Gay Lynch

Departures

Sinead O'Connor waits at the bus stop. Sky swollen and dark, it's pouring with rain. Water courses the gutter, umbrella helpless. She's drenched but grinning, bald head, bright eyes, ready to rip up a photo of God or the president or the bus driver if need be. The 8:10 am rounds the corner and she glances back to see your mother, breaking into a run. Sinead laughs and steps up on that threshold of bus—half-in, half-out—until your mother arrives, out of breath, wet and cold. The two move all the way to the back and sit side-by-side in their leather jackets, leaning into each other, whispering. Even hidden, their tattoos glow, illuminating Sinead's chest with Jesus and your mother's arms with all of that bright ink.

Shady Cosgrove

Mother and Daughter

This is a very common dream
about a small girl
        who is walking
            down
a road she can't remember

and the mother
        who paints the name
of the road in the sky
        when the daughter
is too short to reach it.

When the daughter is ten,
      the mother lifts her up

          but,
the daughter is still too short.

'Higher,' the daughter says,
          only
she is HEAVY and the mother
      releases her
         without warning
into
  the second part
      of this very common dream.

Here
  the daughter

begins to walk
              on the tips of her toes
and the mother
climbs onto her shoulders,
                 but
she is HEAVY and the daughter
          releases her
                    without warning
into the final part of this very common dream.

Here
     the daughter
               begins to stretch skyward
                    eager
to read the name of the once unreachable road.

Billie Travalini

Curses

I met with a witch in the hasten of early morning, where beach turns to scrub and the moon can't be seen. She had long skirts and a fox on a lead. I handed her a bottle of mezcal and heirloom prayer beads in return for a spell: I wanted to hurt a ghost.

She stared out at the lifting darkness that could be new-horizon, and I remembered a little girl on the other side of the world, waiting at the bottom of a wooded driveway-long afternoons dimming into dusk.

'How about I sit with you,' the witch said, lowering beside me, onto a piece of driftwood. The fox nestled between, and she held my hand. I could smell the ancient of evergreens and moss.

Shady Cosgrove

Windstorm Mothers

How very dare they? *Windstorm mothers.*
Where will we be if there is widespread protest?
Keep the pact and shut-the-fuck-up about it!

Julia Prendergast

Initiations

For my tenth birthday you gave me a ghetto blaster with two Madonna cassette tapes. I marched round the yard with that Sony sound speaker on my shoulder, shouting out to materialism. Circling the house, I pranced the uneven grass, stepping round your boyfriend's pick-up, ever-patient on cement blocks. Or maybe it was those breath-cloud mornings, when we'd pray for the car to start so we could get my sister to the ferry dock for school, the three of us singing Joan Baez at full tilt. Or that Dolly vinyl in your cupboard—she's wearing heels and carrying a paint roller—singing about working hours and immigrants. Culture is the common sense you take for granted. Country longing and regret, folk grief, rock and roll lust.

Shady Cosgrove

Not Like an Uncle

Attempting to describe her sixteen-year-old daughter's new boss at the ice-cream shop, my sister says he is sort of like an uncle—he's kind, and treats all the casual staff so well. But then her face sours, like she's slurped the Lisbon lemon gelato too fast. Quick-smart she corrects herself. *Not like an uncle*, she says, *but you know what I mean.*

Rebekah Clarkson

Thirty Years

At twelve I saw in absolutes.

I wanted to make you happy, set my hands to work transforming you—glamorous as the movie stars you loved, strong-jawed and regal in a Gloria Swanson sort of way.

Perhaps it was in the wanting that I failed. It was only a small favour after all.

Please, you whispered.

My arms hung like broken wings at my sides. I was straitjacketed.

For many moons it was easy believing my failure was a fluke, a lapse in judgment.

Thirty-plus years have passed since that hot August night.

Billie Travalini

The Night Runners

For the whole of grade five, my mother and I lived in Adam's house. All through that winter I lay awake in the wooden bed that once belonged to another little girl, listening as the night runners got ready. Flashes of bright light from their head torches would swish across the bottom of my door as the night runners fussed with shoes and zippers, one last toilet stop. I'd strain for my mother's voice in the rhythmic chanting as the front door clicked behind them, blankets clutched to my chin, the shimmery prickling, always at the back of my neck: the anticipation of being left alone for the next short while. If I was brave enough to leave the bed, I'd watch from my window as they thrummed the road in singular file. They'd puff hot air into the cold—Adam up front, always followed by my mother. Night-running was 'non-negotiable' (I've read Adam's manifesto on the internet).

My mother says it was a fox that led her back to herself. She saw it on a run. Lightning quick, it caught her eye and leapt into an auburn assemblé, a soundless landing, crouching tableau, before disappearing into dusk. Later, she said she'd felt the fox's leap viscerally, as though she was one with the fox, as though she *was* the fox.

We were out of Adam's house in two days. But that frisson of excitement and strangeness, even now, sometimes at night, I crave it. That prickling across the back of my neck.

Rebekah Clarkson

Failings

She was slender as ever by the time I next saw her, only stretch marks—inch-long silver scars, running in diagonals across her hips, shore-lining her nipples.

Julia Prendergast

Communities

Golden Orb I

Golden orbs canopy the woods overhead: black and yellow bodies, long legs. They seem poised, comfortable with taking up space. There's more and more, I realise—a new web every few feet, along the handrail, between bushes, sunlight glinting off white strands. The spiders set up close to each other—but not too close. Off the trail, in the sunlight, huge gauzy nets span trees with ten or fifteen spiders all connected, maybe more. I look this up: proximity for protection and food, social means. Perhaps they have retired together, here, near the ocean, checking in on each other and sharing meals so they're not a burden on their children.

Golden Orb II

Golden orbs canopy the woods overhead, close but not too close. Proximity for protection and food, for social means. Perhaps the golden orb is a model for living with this unconventional love: separate webs, occasional sociability.

Golden Orb III

A group of spiders is called a clutter or a cluster. Clutter seems unfair, cluster too astral, though spiders do suspend star-like in the air. Perhaps a commune of spiders.

Shady Cosgrove

J is for Jellyfish

Lou's eyes flick up to the rear vision mirror, her son's four-year-old wispy head, oblivious between the soft padded wings of his car seat.

She checks the mirror again, catching Jay's eye as he throws his head from side to side.

'I spy with my little eye, sumpfink beginning with J!'

Lou thrums the steering wheel, her eyes on the shimmering endless road. Terracotta dirt flanks both sides, dotted with random bushes, tiny red rocks, a pale silvery white sky above—full desert. She drops her eyes to the petrol gauge, visualises the jerry can and bottles of water in the boot. There's probably a ratio she should have considered more carefully, one adult and a child, distance between roadhouses, required hydration.

'Um … okay. Let's see.'

J is for jerry can. J is for juice—she hadn't packed any and he was going to want some soon.

'C'mon Mummy!'

'Ahhh. Oh, gosh. That's a hard one, mate. Mummy can't see anything starting with J. Give me a minute.'

Cackling from the booster seat, veering into unhinged.

She starts to feel a new level of panic, no longer the petrol or the water …

'Jumper?'

'No!' he shrieks. More thrashing his head back and forth.

Random jumpers had been stuffed into suitcases. She hadn't even checked—was it cold in Perth?

'Um, umm hang on.' Her mind is blank. 'Jellyfish…!'

Shrieking from the back seat now.

'Okay, I give up.' Her voice cracks. She stretches her arm back, taps his foot. 'Tell me, matey.'

'Me, silly!'

Lou inhales sharply, stretches her eyes to wide open, clenches her mouth.

'Ahhh, of course. You! My beautiful Jay Jay!'

Giggling from the back seat.

Lou keeps her eyes on the road, the middle white lines hypnotic.

When she checks the mirror again, she sees that Jay has fallen asleep, his head tilted back, his small pink mouth open and wet.

Rebekah Clarkson

Twilight Trace

The pine table sits snug beneath the balcony window. Only you will remember its pleasing symmetry, how you pulled your notebook from the bottom drawer, opened it to the last pages, weeping a little as you wrote.

Fauré's 'Pie Jesu' swells the air, fat with sorrow. You lean into it without wallowing. Today's air smells musty—not a hint of fennel nor anise.

Dark crags reflect in the glass of the dormer shutters, fanning in a triptych. Terracotta roof tiles block a clear view of the harbour boats. Only the tips of masts appear. The clock in the tower glows amber.

Ancient Achlys will come for you, spraying mist as she skims across the silk surface of the harbour, rising into the indigo sky before approaching the balcony. Only you and darkness— waiting expectantly for her wisp and slide through the lace of the balustrade.

Below the plane tree on the parelia old men murmur over backgammon and tsipouro. Thin cats drape their bodies across windowsills; basil plants release their sharpness; a girl shouts about ice cream sploshing but you no longer care about messy fetishes.

Scattered across the bed, pages of your manuscript. Futile attempts to capture beauty. You had feared not finishing. In agony, you gather pages and fling them towards the harbour. Watch them flutter far short of the shore.

Asterisks mark your wish for flute and pipe—Threnos dancing, pastries, wine, deletion of digital mess. To remain supine on bleached coverlet, until caïque and tide take you home.

Writerly thrash and hullabaloo. The room explodes with colour. Grim Morphean dreams break. Your head swings in fright—Achlys's mist blinding you.

As she leaves, you note the wettened eyes, surmise her cynicism. Those who come after will remember only a photograph of the scene taken by Kritharas Devienne. Memories build and dissolve—copies, then traces.

Gay Lynch

Why?

How is it we can leave behind some of the lives we might have lived, but not others?

Why do the possibilities of not-lived moments force the self-construction of an *I* that everyone seems to recognise as me, *except* me?

Julia Prendergast

Anticipation

We're inside the lead singer's chest watching the crowd, and we're inside the crowd, watching the lead singer. A simultaneous pulse of heart and audience. The smell of sweat and alcohol and cut grass. I climb onto your shoulders as the lights come up and her/our voice takes stage.

Shady Cosgrove

Five Reasons

Miranda remembers the day in her son's new apartment, how Jacob had looked at her sideways, flattened his lips, and then—full lecturer mode—launched into the reasons. There'd been five. She had tried to imagine her son's students, watching him, as she was then.

She focusses on the memory of Jacob's voice, counting through the reasons—presses her fingers silently into her thigh, throngs of strangers pushing against her, everyone heading in the same direction, for the river.

She has one and two but can't remember the third. The fourth is obvious and so is the fifth.

'That's okay', she'd said that day. 'I'll find my own grandkids. I'll pinch my friends' grandkids. Strangers' grandkids!' Jacob had smiled, moved toward the couch, rubbed the top of her arm with his thumb, so quickly she wasn't sure he had. She remembers he'd been standing by the window. Chrome buildings appeared to sit on each of his shoulders, reminding her of those photos people used to frame of Pisa. The soft, deep couch in his lovely apartment. 'Of course,' she'd added, 'I understand, darling.'

Darling Jacob.

Someone treads on Miranda's toe. The pain shoots straight into her hip, though she doesn't make a sound. Remembering the third reason, she brings the palm of her hand to her heart, presses hard.

Rebekah Clarkson

Punishment from God

Headline: Alabama Senator Calls Hurricane Punishment from God

Pulling onto Bourbon Street Katrina lifts a watery claw, knowing every moment depends on the moment before. The x's and y's. *Always* in that order.

Billie Travalini

Thanks. No.

Bollards block boulevard access.
Giant screens. Summer haze.
Debut music-journo gig. For our Gabe.
'We don't want to go with him, Mum.'
'Listen sprout. No sabotage.'
'We won't have fun with you there.'
'How could you not? At a music concert?'

Massed in the platz, not ready to mosh.
Me and my sister, slowcore,
slouch-louching in the crowd.
Heads a-sly-swivel, fan-girling.
Standing room only tickets.
From the balcony, a rustle and rush.
A fierce girl leans out, sings up her grief.

Dress aqua baby-doll, expression bleak.
Gamin high fringe, pink streaks.
Blood tears, illuminati eyes.
Mouth over her mic. Like she'll bite it.
After an hour of sweats and wails,
she plucks out pills, poked into tampons.
I pull a phial of scotch from my boot. Alto sax.

Munted, we sway, holding hands,
drifting forward, plunking faux guitars.
Sistering. Ululatin' to a backbeat.
A crowd compressed and mournful.
By the second set, mood crackling.

Shoved, we stagger. Struggle for breath.
Gabe seizes my arm and hauls me up.
'Try to stay upright. Fuckity. Don't fall.'
Mass moves like a wave, we go under.
He shouts at us, 'Legs astride, balance.'
Head swimming, I download his full lecture,
until I'm swept away from him.
'If you can't get up,' he shouts,
'curl your body on the ground,
cradle your most precious organ.'
Pop-eyed, on my knees.
'Pull in your head, like a turtle.
Or they'll smash it to shell grit.
Grind you under their boots.
Fat boys will deflate your lungs when they land.'

Hands on his head, face screwed,
he recounts all this to our mother.
The crowd. How we went down.
How twice he fished us out like rubbish bags.
How we fucked up his first assignment.
We say, 'Thank you. Big love.' Yawn.

Gay Lynch

Befuddled

How hard we work to save ourselves
from ourselves—that part of us that goes
so far back names are forgotten, worn
smooth as the tombstones we leave
in our wake, like Napoleon who headed
from Corsica to Elba—misguided the way we
all are when we are stuck in the middle.
'Ambition is never content.'
This is what Napoleon wanted us to know,
wanted us to understand, lest we fall short,
befuddled, not by the pluses or the minuses of taking
one road and not another, but by something far more insidious:
Qui … qui suis-je? Who … am I?

Billie Travalini

Banished

This island is for wind-listeners—my banished-self and present-
selves, side by side.

Julia Prendergast

The Buck's Party

Tom thought the buck's party was going well enough. He smiled over at Levi, who seemed to be having a good time, although it was hard to tell because he was a guy who would say his buck's party was awesome no matter what. Tom knew in his heart that this party was not awesome. Energy was low at 8 pm. At least they weren't eating dinner too early, which would have been daggy. Timing the spit roast had caused Tom some anxiety. As best man, he had done all the thinking, all the planning, though Joel had helped. It wasn't as if he was going to arrange for a stripper; the guys from church weren't into anything like that. Jason was here, which couldn't really be helped—he *was* part of the group. His sandy hair crusted with salt and clumped around his hunched shoulders in a way that Tom found repulsive: Jason would never find a wife. But then, neither had Tom.

He cued 'upbeat anthems' for the next playlist, turned up the volume.

Tom's mum had given him her recipe for potato salad and the guys were commenting on how good it was. Finely chopped gherkins were the key. Tom explained this to the guys and they all laughed together about their mums' salad recipes.

Joel was further out on the balcony talking to his wife, dipping his chin low to his chest as though he were creating a private space.

As Toto's 'Africa' came on, Tom cranked the volume. He watched as Joel turned and jogged down to the beach with his phone, away from the guys, the drums of 'Africa' picking up behind him.

Tom watched Joel talking intently into his phone as he paced the shoreline. Tom thought of Joel's wife, Amy, home alone with the baby, maybe crying over her shoulder. A strange feeling came over Tom, imagining Joel's wife like that, and he became alarmed, suddenly, that he couldn't control his face, crumpling. He forced his eyes over Joel's head to the horizon line, focussing all his energy there, remembering the advice from when he was carsick as a kid. The guys filled their plates with lamb and salad and Tom stood like that till the feeling passed.

Rebekah Clarkson

Negotiations

Music drifts through my window—after each song there's a pause, then applause. Something is uttered. I can't make it out. I picture the stage—singer with a microphone, people sitting at quiet tables, some standing, pushing towards the front. This is how we've taken to communicating. All-day concerts outside each other's windows. Aural postcards. Eavesdropping on the late summer.

Shady Cosgrove

In Love

I LOVE her.

I'm in love with her.

I want to be her memory-worker.

Julia Prendergast

What's the point?

Later, much later, I thought about telling you I slept with your brother for most of our marriage. To this day, it's the not telling that bothers me. Then again, I remember all the times you said you knew me better than I knew myself. Anyway, after much therapy—more than a little soul searching—I decided I won't list all the ways Tom made me feel better than you ever did. What's the point?

Billie Travalini

Prison Dreaming

The night before I left Melbourne, I dreamt I was packing a bag to go to prison. For *speeding*. It sounds made up because, of course, dreams are. *However.* Dreams are far from nothing.

Julia Prendergast

People are Weird

From the cockpit, the captain tells us we've reached 40,000 feet, can unbuckle our seatbelts if we wish. Our flight attendant—Stacey—strolls the aisle, glancing left to right.

From 24E, I notice that a guy sitting up ahead has taken the laminated snacks menu from the seat pocket in front, folded it in halves and halves again and propped it on his tray table—a makeshift holder for his phone.

When Stacey arrives at 20C, she leans over the guy, tortoise shell glasses perched on her nose, and tells him loudly, 'It's *not okay* to bend our menus like that.'

The way Stacey says 'our menus' makes me want to stay on her plane forever.

I hear the man protest, like a belligerent child: 'It's only *one*.'

Stacey stands tall, strides to the back of the plane—her smart blue skirt skims the back of my hand.

I feel the frisson of an interchange and then two young women appear from the front, trolley cart in-tow.

Wheels lock at 20C.

The flight attendant sporting a smart bob says something sharp into the guy's ear, snatches up the mangled menu, pushes it into her cart. When she gets to me, placing a little brown paper napkin on my tray, the cutest packet of mixed nuts, I catch her eye and say, 'Thank you so much.' She smiles back, squints her hazel-flecked perfect eyes. 'People are weird,' she says, and opens her eyes wide. Her lips are a deep matte red and I nod, *yes*.

Eventually, the guy at 20C falls asleep, his head lolls to one side, mouth slack. I stay awake the entire flight, hands in my lap.

Rebekah Clarkson

Reality

Are we more, or less, culpable if we live in absenteeism?

I feel defunct, as if reality is only a construction in my mind's eye.

Julia Prendergast

Ode to Writers' Necks

Dear neck. Heads have never been the whole point.
As a writer, sedentary, solitary, I love to work.
To hunch and sprawl over digital and paper texts.
Page and screen hooked. All-nighters. Guilty.

Most writers can't live off their words.
Publishers preferencing popular. More
pointless pressure on necks, practising Homo erectus.
Next Homo sapiens—write, rewrite, think upstairs.

In the head, the house, on the heath, stay grounded.
'Live on the land,' neck says. 'I've got your back. And your head.'
I heave hay bales, battle rogue bulls, teeter in tree forks, chainsaw dangling,
shape logs from branches and trunks, to saw, chop, stack, incinerate, hose
and rake. Neck, I love you.

Human infants take a year to support their heads in locomotion,
a feat achieved by other animals soon after birth. Brain weight. Dead weight.
Were it not for necks, the business end of spines, writers would be extinct.

Neck, with respect, sincere thanks.
For furniture shifted, house moves, supermarket bags lugged.
With little kids at foot, tugging on my small frame.
'Always do your share,' Mother said.
Neck, dear sherpa, I'm grateful for your altitude.

Head-first, spine strong, I go, from chair to desk, page to paddock.
To tenderly curve around an anxious man, a nursing babe, a tearful teen, friend
after friend exploited by men. Oh, neck. Now you're in pain?

Our family weighed down by worry, stoop a bit.
We exercise to release endorphins.
To build muscle, to work harder, longer, smarter.
Suddenly you, neck, squark 'enough.'
Decade after decade, not a peep.
Excuses come. Bullying, one more run. I need to stay strong.

Who knew how much a neck hates to leap, to kick-box,
to push-up, to squat, on repeat, to run kilometre after kilometre.
The nightly wrestle of rubber pillows that leave neck hanging.
Cervicothoracic junction of arteries, facets and joints
jacking up, crying out over fifty-five kilos. Oh no.
X-ray report. Widespread bone and disc degenerative change.

Arthritis colonises all necks over forty. Only thirty percent radiate pain.
After four months—prognosis chronic.
Medical man says, 'You're fucked. Nothing can be done.'
Writer me dreams of drugs and massages, physios, miraculous cure.
'Your neck will pain you the rest of your life. An indisputable fact,' he adds.
I switch to hemp gummies. Stick my head in the sand.

Gay Lynch

Tightrope

My father embarrasses me with his showing off. I want him to act like other fathers. I don't dare say anything because I know my mother worries about him as much as I do, even though she never lets on.

'At least he makes people smile,' she says.

It's an awful thing to say. Just once I want her to admit she's as embarrassed as I am.

I think about all this as my father grabs the pole he bought at Greenburg Plumbing Supplies and climbs through the attic window towards a rope stretched to my tree house like a clothesline without any clothes.

I step forward. My eyes are shut.

Behind me my mother is clapping.

Billie Travalini

Grief

Grief I

The anger–sad moves in a slow ricochet from chest to belly and then back again. I think of bar-tailed godwits, flying the Pacific Ocean without stopping: America to New Zealand, then up through Asia and back. They're waders, not sea birds, but they migrate anyway, feeding as they fly. My torso, an ocean. These feelings, determined birds.

Grief II

The godwits do not resent the ocean its girth.

Grief III

Two godwits (compassion and unattachment) fly the perimeter of what is possible. I feel my scapula as wings.

Shady Cosgrove

Best Day Ever

I was feeling grateful and also bad because my sister had abruptly left work after I'd sobbed down the phone that my husband's GP had rung to say that he was concerned for my husband's safety and would not let him drive home alone but would send him to hospital in an ambulance, which my husband had begged him not to do, unless I was able to pick him up, which of course I wasn't, because our only car was now at the doctor's surgery. I found my husband alone in a room with the door not closed but also not open. My sister gave me a wink from the waiting area as my husband and I went back into the GP's room. He talked in circles until I also agreed that the mental health care system was indeed broken. My sister then drove my husband back to her house while I bought lunch from a nearby café, thinking and thinking about what I should do next. The three of us sat in the sun in my sister's backyard eating organic salads with the final remnants of a tree that had fallen over in last year's storm, making my sister cry, wondering how long it had lived there, before us. I was still trying to work out what to do next when I turned to my sister, said: 'Thank you so much for helping us, for leaving work, dropping everything.' My sister looked at me with the calm smile that is distinctively hers, turned to my husband, and cocked an eyebrow. 'Best day ever.'

Rebekah Clarkson

Snap

Snap to all of it: migraine headaches, pulsing void of missing things, embodied and unnameable.

Julia Prendergast

Restoration Project

Elbows draped over balcony rail, Mother smokes. We set off then with backpacks, Cochinillo sandwiches and flasks of tea, for the Roman aqueduct, a 200-metre walk. The place where Father left us.

Wind bites our necks bared by blunt haircuts. Mother's eyes water. On the steep ascent, we encounter the famous brass devil with whom visitors take selfies. In Segovia's story, a girl climbs high to bring water home in a pail. Each time, she deals with the Devil.

If she relinquishes her soul, he'll build her an aqueduct. I rock on my heels, imagine water splashing from her heavy bucket, metal abrading her legs on the way down—her flawed freedom.

Mother lags. I rush towards the structure, impossibly high, gracefully curved. Built with granite and no mortar, it carries water sixteen kilometres from the Frio River to the city. Does her engineering heart sing?

'Slaves died stacking these rocks,' she says, grim-faced.

'Father told me Romans invented concrete.'

'Pwssht!' she replies.

I will not say aloud that I know he jumped.

'Grieving over modern slaves in Masdar City.' Mother broods on Father. 'Something happened to him out there.'

On the edge of the cobbled path, knees dissolving, I calculate the drop, burrow my head in Mother's coat. It smells of cigarette smoke and patchouli, lapels wet with tears. She sways, as if she can't take the hardness and height anymore, as if something thousands of years old could not have so many consequences.

Mother consults away from Segovia because of Father. Every spring, we leave flowers at the site and then I tug her away.

I think how the Devil built it before cockcrow. About dirty deals. About me playing *Assassin's Creed* with Father and how he pretended to love parkour. Had the aqueduct climb unbalanced him? I felt not. Drunk or sad? No-one in their right mind would climb it.

Gay Lynch

Windbreaks

I hold my breath underwater, consider epiphanies, windbreaks—

Julia Prendergast

Family Violence

Suppertime we decorate our gingkoes with amber lights.
Wee girl pushes through our brush fence.
Sticks in her hair. Eyes swollen black.
Maude cranks up our cello to cover the girl's groans.

Hollyhocks screen gaps between our households.
Blooms nod. Door slams, truck revs, gravel screeches.
Bloke never discerns observation. Goes off. Right off.
Nothing registers outside his righteous rage.

Jacoba tends weeping skin flaps, bruise maps.
Womanish, Tadeus stands at our backs; forgets nothing.
Wields tortoiseshell hairbrush through girl's blood clots.
Knuckles clenched he helps her limp home.

First time, we carry our custards sweating beneath calico.
Next, Royale duck eggs to ward off evil eyes.
Third time, in steaming pot, pookies for our perpetrator.
Bestow upon him thumping pixie visions.

Mother once said, choose loamy black shrooms.
Heavy in the bucket. Grit taste. As required.
At burial, girl selective mute, yet stands tall like new.
Him dug in so deep, our spades hit bracky water.

Silver birch and flax flowers cure contaminated soil.
Under wee woman's shawl, bowl of a belly looms.
Our household durst not utter the devil's name.
Thady cautions patience, learned from life.

Tiny mewling thing possesses neither
darkling brows nor needy-greedy mouth.
Only the girl's knowledge. Strength.
Should malfeasant kin turn up,
we shall keep wee mother and babe safe.

Gay Lynch

Annihilation

The outside haunts in. Ivy creeps inside my bedroom window, weaves tendrils through spaces invisible. Annihilates my belief it's truly possible to cultivate a reclusive life.

Julia Prendergast

Opportunity

Beloved Elder, that's what she calls me. She's telling the AA meeting about her spreadsheet. I don't say anything—of course not—but inside I'm rolling my eyes. Google Docs and spreadsheets, what's next? We'll sign up for shifts, she says, and look after our Beloved Elder.

Surgery like this is everyday and once-in-a-lifetime. Maybe twice, if you go back for the other hip.

And now I'm flat on the daybed, unable to pee by myself, and staring up through a skylight I built into the roof once-upon-a-time forty years ago. Two husbands and three kids ago. Nothing to do but watch those airplanes straight-lining it across the blue.

And those spreadsheet names are now people, sitting by the fireplace, telling me how they get through their days. Skateboard father-of-two. Pantsuit hospital administrator. Uber driver-waitress.

I used to be judgy in meetings—you hear some doozies—but stories belong to people and they're the ones bringing meals, checking my bandage. Maybe, too, there's something about names. I'm going to be worthy of this one, wear it like a fur across my shoulders. Something to keep this old body warm when the dark sets in.

Shady Cosgrove

Your voice

Your voice is becoming indistinguishable from one of my own.

Julia Prendergast

Diesel

Wooden front door in need of a scrape, sand, and polish. Cobwebbed, dried-out garden beds and forgotten left over piles of rubble. A screen side-door, dark and musty inside. I give it a rattle. A dishevelled older woman in a t-shirt and knickers appears. I sense I am her first human on this day. She tells me she isn't even dressed yet.

Susan is up in the horse sheds. She faces me in her dark wrap sunglasses, stands perfectly still as I approach. A long plait of greying blonde hair snakes out from a trucker's cap. Skinny white legs, black shorts with pockets, a vinyl bum bag.

'I knocked on the front door,' I say, and gesture back up to the house. She scrunches her eyebrows and pulls in her chin, looks at me sideways. 'Wouldn't it be obvious where I'd be?'

Every horse in Susan's herd is her favourite. She tells each of them this as they nuzzle her face and neck. Diesel took years to trust her, she tells me. That one taught *her* about trust. This one is the leader: see how they all give him space, move around him?

Diesel is a brilliant chestnut, sparkling with flecks of quartz. Susan directs me to the bend of his ears, the shape and sound of his nostrils, hang of his head, the deep black pools of his eyes, flinching in his flank, texture of his tail, the quality of his smallest musculature. 'This is how you *listen* to a horse,' Susan says. 'You can't ride if you don't know how to listen.'

I rub my hand across Diesel's body—his neck, tops of legs, belly. 'See that,' Susan says, 'that flinch? You just hit a sore spot.' I withdraw my hand, quickly. I tell Susan I won't touch that spot again. 'No, no,' says Susan, 'you *should* touch that sore spot. Massage that spot.'

I lift my hand again, place it on the bottom of Diesel's neck and knead my fingers gently into gristle. Susan points to the raised veins popping up on Diesel's neck. 'See that,' she says. 'That's blood flow. That's healing.'

Rebekah Clarkson

Wind

What I'll miss when I'm dead, presuming we are capable of missing bodily things: the wind on my face.

Julia Prendergast

Acknowledgements

Thank you to Shane Strange, Publisher at Recent Work Press, for publishing this book and, more broadly, for his expansive vision. We admire your compass, particularly your celebration of short from prose, narrative lyricism, poetry, and hybrid forms of writing.

We thank Catherine Collins and Rowena Kidd for their generosity and astute proofreading.

Stories in this collection have appeared elsewhere, sometimes in a slightly different form. We are grateful to the editors of the following publications:

Rebekah Clarkson's 'Best Day Ever' was first published in *The Constancy of Woodpigeons, Bath Flash Fiction* Volume Nine, (Ad Hoc Fiction, UK, 2024).

Rebekah Clarkson's 'Leaving in Four' was first published in *Fish Anthology 2024* (Fish Publishing, Ireland, 2025).

Rebekah Clarkson's 'The Night Runners' was first published in *How it Works: The Uniqueness of the Short Story*, eds. Maurice A. Lee and Aaron Penn, (Lee and Penn Publishing, 2025).

Gay Lynch's 'Red Brain: Red Games' was first published in T*he Writing Mind: Creative Writing Responses to Images of the Living Brain,* eds. Julia Prendergast, Eileen Herbert-Goodall & Jen Webb, (Canberra: Recent Work Press, 2023).

Julia Prendergast's contributions were first published in *Blent*, (Spineless Wonders | Short Australian Stories, 2025).

About the Authors

Rebekah Clarkson is the author of *Barking Dogs* (Affirm Press), a short story cycle set on Peramangk land, South Australia. Her stories have been recognised in major awards in Australia and overseas, including the ABR Elizabeth Jolley Short Story Prize, the Fish Publishing Short Story Prize, and the Bath Flash Fiction Award. Her work has appeared in publications including *Griffith Review, Best Australian Stories* and *Something Special, Something Rare: Outstanding Short Stories* by Australian Women (Black Inc.). Her short memoir, 'Dominion', was recently published in *The Louisville Review*. Rebekah has been awarded residencies at Varuna, The National Writers' House, the Tyrone Guthrie Centre at Annaghmakerrig and the Farrera Art and Nature Centre. She's taught creative writing at several Australian universities, the University of Texas at Austin and as guest lecturer at the University of Cambridge. She works as a senior academic learning adviser at Adelaide University.

Shady Cosgrove writes on Dharawal land and teaches creative writing at the University of Wollongong, Australia. Her most recent book *Flight* (Gazebo Books 2024), explores the linked tensions of flight and longing, and her short works and articles have appeared in *Best Australian Stories, Anthology of Australian Prose Poetry, Dreaming Awake, New Writing, TEXT, The Scholarship of Creative Writing Practice, Animal Studies Journal, The Writing Mind, Cordite, Overland, Antipodes, Southerly, Island, takahe* and *the Eunoia Review*. She's received an ANU HRC Fellowship, a Bundanon Artists Residency and the Varuna House Eleanor Dark Flagship Fellowship. For more information, see www. shadycosgrove.com.

Gay Lynch writes essays, novels, and stories on unceded Bunurong land and adjunct to Flinders University. In 2025, she judged the Creative Prose Prize, AAALS (American Association Australasian Literary Studies), which she had won in 2024, and Rebekah Clarkson launched Lynch's debut collection *Hebe's Lament & Other Stories* at the 17th ICSSE (International Conference on the Short Story in English), in Killarney, Ireland. In 2023, Lynch presented on flash, delivered a paper, and read at the 16th ICSSE in Singapore; read for APWT (Australian Pacific Writers & Translators) at the Ubud Writers and Readers' Festival; and chaired panels at the 2023 ASSF (Australian Short Story Festival). In 2019, she launched Unsettled, at ISAANZ (Irish Studies Association of Australia and New Zealand).

Julia Prendergast lives in Melbourne on unceded Wurundjeri land. She is a fiction writer, essayist, and prose poet, with a particular interest in realist forms of writing, as well as fractured and experimental prose. Her novel, *The Earth Does Not Get Fat* was longlisted for the Indie Book Awards (debut fiction). *Bloodrust and Other Stories* was published in 2022 (fiction of the week: SMH and *The Age* newspapers). *Blent* will be published in 2025. Julia's stories and prose poems have been recognised and published in *Lightship Anthology* (UK), *Glimmer Train* (US), Séan Ó Faoláin Competition (IE), *New Writing* (UK), *TEXT* (AU). Her essays are published in *New Writing*, and elsewhere. Julia is Associate Professor and Discipline Leader (Creative Writing, Literature, and Publishing) at Swinburne University. She is a practice-led researcher with a particular interest in neuro|psychoanalytic approaches to creative writing. Julia is President/Chair of the Australasian Association of Writing Programs (AAWP), the peak academic body representing the discipline of Creative Writing (Australasia).

Billie Travalini, a fiction and nonfiction writer, lives in the United States. Her area of focus is the voice—a commitment to including voices who are often left out of the conversation. Her work has been published in *The Moth, Another Chicago Magazine, Remnants, The Lakeview International Journal of Literature and Art,* as well as numerous anthologies. Her memoir, *Blood Sisters*, was a finalist for the Breadloaf Prize and won the Lewes Clark Discovery Prize. Billie received the Governor's Award for the Arts, the Delaware Division of the Arts Masters Award in Literature, and the National Federation of Press Women Communicator of Achievement Award. After a successful career as a journalist, Billie has taught at Temple University and Lincoln University. She currently teaches at Wilmington University.

About the Cover Art and Artist

Embrace by Margaret Ambridge

The artwork *Embrace* was made in response to conversations I had with women about aging, how they navigate their own mortality and the 'gendered shame' of ageing. I asked them if they were more fearful of looking old than the inevitability of getting old. Many of the women I interviewed spoke of the mirror:

I have conversations with myself in the mirror—I am bigger than you.

It is so much more empowering to embrace it—I have to deal with it.

I walk away from the mirror and remember who I am (or what I was).

I have been a long time like that, and only a short time like this—it is still fresh enough at this end to remember what I used to look like in the mirror.

I am acutely aware of my muses' vulnerability, what they share with me and the risks they take. I am forever grateful. Being visible and relevant can be and should be life-long.

Margaret Ambridge, 2025

Margaret Ambridge is a multidisciplinary artist living and working on Kaurna land. Margaret works with drawing, sculpture, installation, photography and video. She has been a finalist in, and winner of many national art prizes. Her works explore the liminal spaces of the human condition, its fears, loves and taboos, the difficult conversational and experiential places we avoid. To deepen connection, Margaret regularly adapts materials that have already had a life such as bed linen, clothing, dress makers' patterns, and tree bark. Her tonal approach involves endless charcoal marks and subsequent erasure. The method

is slow, the passage of time allowing her to examine her own
responses to complex conversations, to question the boundaries
we place on each other and our environments.

www.ingramcontent.com/pod-product-compliance
Lightning Source LLC
Chambersburg PA
CBHW061459210726
48287CB00007B/2581